The Adventures of Rexie and Tigey

By Candice Rudolph

Dedicated to.

The little boy who made a once upon a time little girls dream of becoming a published author a reality.

Someday, you will realize just what the reality of being blessed with you did for my soul.

You will forever be my baby, my child, my heart, my lovey, my son, my sunshine... MY MONKEY!

I love you all the way past heaven, back down to earth & into your heart!

I know, I know, we LOVE each other the SAME!

A Mamasuarus Publication

Words copyrighted to Candice Rudolph 2022

Illustrations copyrighted to Doodley Bobz 2022

Rexie
forgets
his
stuffy

Rexie is going to the
park to meet
some friends today
and can't decide
what to wear.

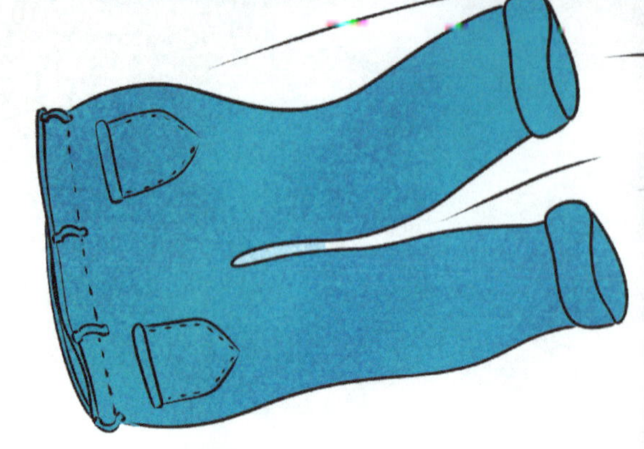

"Why don't you wear these?"
Momma asks as she hands Rexie his favorite pair of red shorts.

"Momma, you always think ahead and make things better. Thanks Momma". Rexie says as he squeezes her tightly.

"That's because I'm
SUPER MOMMA!
I'm here to save the day"

Momma laughs as she
swoops down
and twirls Rexie in
the air.

Rexie quickly gets dressed and
runs outside to meet
his friends.
"Come on Momma, I don't want
to be the last one at the park"
he yells as he hops around
waiting for Momma.

Momma grabs her bag,
walks outside and takes
Rexie's claw.
"Are you sure you have
everything Monkey?" she asks.
"I sure do" Rexie says and pulls
Momma by the claw.

When they arrive at the park,
Rexie rushes off
to the playground to
play with his friends,
leaving Momma
with the other grown-ups.

Rexie's friends all have
their stuffy's.
Rexie quickly realizes he
was in such a hurry to see his
friends, he forgot
his own stuffy.
"Momma, Momma, I forgot Tigey"
he cries as he runs to Momma.

Momma wipes Rexie's tears.
"Don't cry Monkey, I have
something special for you"
she says as she pulls his stuffy
out of her bag.
"Momma, you brought Tigey!
Thank you, Thank you"
Rexie says.

"We should always think of others and how our actions make them feel.

I knew forgetting Tigey would make you sad, and bringing him would make you happy.

So I grabbed him" Momma says smiling.

Rexie runs off to show his
friends Tigey, but quickly
stops to pick a flower.
"I thought of you as I ran to
my friends and how this
flower would make you happy.
So I picked it for you Momma"
he says.

"I love you Momma"
Rexie says hugging Tigey.
"I love you more Monkey"
Momma says hugging Rexie.